The Human Cannonball's Last Thought

And Other Funny Circus Poems

by

J. Thomas Sparough

Illustrated by
Rachael Griffin

Space Painter Publications
Cincinnati, Ohio

Space Painter Publications
4228 Delaney Street
Cincinnati, Ohio 45223
(513) 542-1231
SpacePainter.com

Printed in the United States of America
130616

ISBN: 9-780977-290239

Contents:

Baby Pachyderm 6

My Robot Juggler 8

The Human Cannonball's Last Thought 10

My Grandma is the Weight Lifter 12

A Gorilla Got Loose 14

I'm Not a Babysitter 16

Dinner Show 18

Australian Star 20

Trixie 22

Best View 24

My Boy Ran Away to the Circus 27

Clown Prayer 28

Zebra 30

Smile 32

Guest Star 34

I Sell Hot Dogs 36

I Sell Snow Cones 39

I Wish My Dad 40

Inside the Lion's Jaws 42

Man-Eating Tigers 45

The Unseen Pro 46

Hair Twister 48

Dad's the Ringmaster 50

High Wire Dare 52

Librarian's Pet 54

The Snake Charmer 56

The Littlest Show on Earth 58

The Smallest 60

Dedications:

I dedicate this to my mother.
I wouldn't have wanted any other.

She could pick up a glass from the top
in a backbend without spilling a drop.

Of course, the glass was empty,
but I sure thought it nifty.

J. Thomas Sparough

To my parents for their
unconditional love as they
encouraged my childhood
drawing, even when they
discovered my surprise
masterpieces on the walls
and doors throughout our
house.

Rachael Griffin

Baby Pachyderm

I am baby pachyderm,
who needs to have some fun.
I don't get what happened.
Why did they have to run?

All five hundred people
should not have had to flee.
What the heck's the matter?
Why are they scared of me?

I trotted up the aisle.
The people were in awe.
Suddenly they panicked,
and there was Ma and Pa.

Dad chased me through the seats.
My parents love to play.
Why did the humans scream
and have to run away?

My Robot Juggler

My robot juggler
with sixteen balls
was not programmed
to hear my calls.

"Electric dude!
You better stop.
You're out of cord.
You're gonna drop."

His motor hummed.
He sensed the cheers.
The crowd's applause
just greased his gears.

But the lifeline snapped.
The juice went dead,
and sixteen balls
crashed on his head.

The Human Cannonball's Last Thought

If you really must know,
here's what I am thinking.
I'm stuck in the cannon,
regretting my drinking.

I had a root beer float
and a glass of lemonade,
then a big sip of water
and a jug of Kool-Aid.

But the fuse is now lit.
I've tensed up my body.
Yet all I can think is
"I've got to go potty!"

My Grandma is the Weight Lifter

My grandma is the weight lifter,
strong woman extraordinaire.
She works in the Big Top Circus.
Her poster is everywhere.

She started when she was younger
by baling hay at the farm.
Then later she had six children.
She carried them with one arm.

And now she performs her lifting,
though some say she's gone too far,
by raising a shining auto
with me on top of the car.

A Gorilla Got Loose

A gorilla got loose
at the circus last night
and ran through the stands
to look for a fight.

He pounded his chest
and roared really loud.
He tipped over ten drinks
and glared at the crowd.

But the show did not stop.
So the beast sat right down.
He ordered three hot dogs
and clapped for the clown.

I'm Not a Babysitter

I'm not a babysitter,
but my brother doesn't mind.
While studying my program,
I got into this bind.

My parents went for popcorn,
and Joey left his seat.
He crawled down to an elephant,
who raised him up ten feet.

My parents are returning,
and my brother's in the show.
I won't get any popcorn
if that elephant lets go.

Dinner Show

My climb to work
was not with ease.
I feared my turn
on that trapeze.

My wobbly flip
was nearly missed.
"You eat too much,"
my catcher hissed.

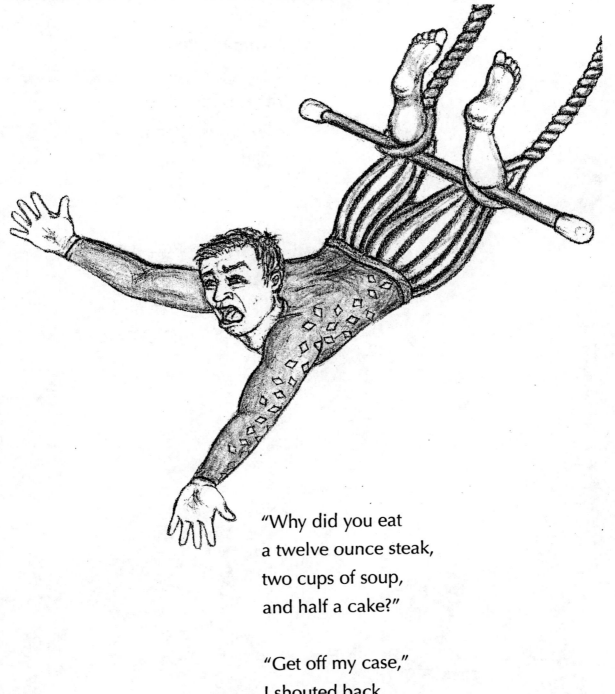

"Why did you eat
a twelve ounce steak,
two cups of soup,
and half a cake?"

"Get off my case,"
I shouted back.
"Or during break,
I'll have a snack."

Australian Star

The Australian star,
who loved to hop,
had done his act
but wouldn't stop.

They tried to grab him.
He was too fast.
They tried the net.
He hopped right past.

They tried to rope him.
He jumped right through.
No one could catch
that kangaroo.

Trixie

Trixie, the amazing
manicured poodle,
pranced to the spotlight
and did a big doodle.

Out came the trainer
holding a hoop,
smiling and waving,
slipped in the...

Best View

If you arrive early
to get the best seat
and sit in the front row,
I've still got you beat.

I see all the antics.
I chuckle and laugh.
I don't need a ticket.
I am a giraffe.

My Boy Ran Away to the Circus

My boy ran away to the circus,
and he was my very best friend.
The sneak crawled into the performance
he wasn't allowed to attend.

And there he watched boys his own age
performing his favorite tricks.
He could hardly wait to try them.
He had always been good with sticks.

He raced down to get to the trainer.
They must have had good dialogue,
because now he has joined the circus,
and he was my very best dog.

Clown Prayer

Please grant that...
My socks won't match.
My nose glows red.
I kiss a frog.
I eat my bed.

Please grant that...
My hat won't fit.
My dog will fly.
I fall right down.
I'm hit by pie.

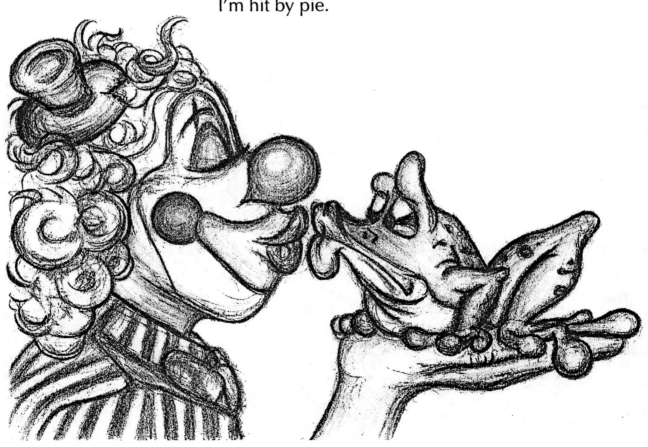

Please grant that...
The people point
and slap their knee,
fall off their chair,
and laugh at me.

Zebra

My zebra has stopped her dancing,
and she used to be so bold.
She caught an unusual sickness
that at first was just a cold.

The medicines don't seem helpful.
She has slipped into a daze.
My zebra has stopped her sniffling,
but her stripes have flipped sideways.

Smile

The funny clown
said, "I should quit.
No one loves me
one tiny bit."

He was a man
with one black boot,
a torn gray hat,
a pin-striped suit.

I waved my arms,
'cause I've been sad,
then smiled at him
to make him glad.

He changed his mind.
I saved the show.
He did not quit.
He seemed aglow.

The spotlight shined
and lit him up.
He dived into
a big teacup.

The people cheered.
His clothes were wet.
His thumbs went up
when our eyes met.

Guest Star

A pigeon flew into the tent
and turned a loop de loop
then stealing center stage with ease
dived through a flaming hoop.

She perched upon the highest pole
as if she owned the tent,
but then she snatched my candy bar
and out the flap she went.

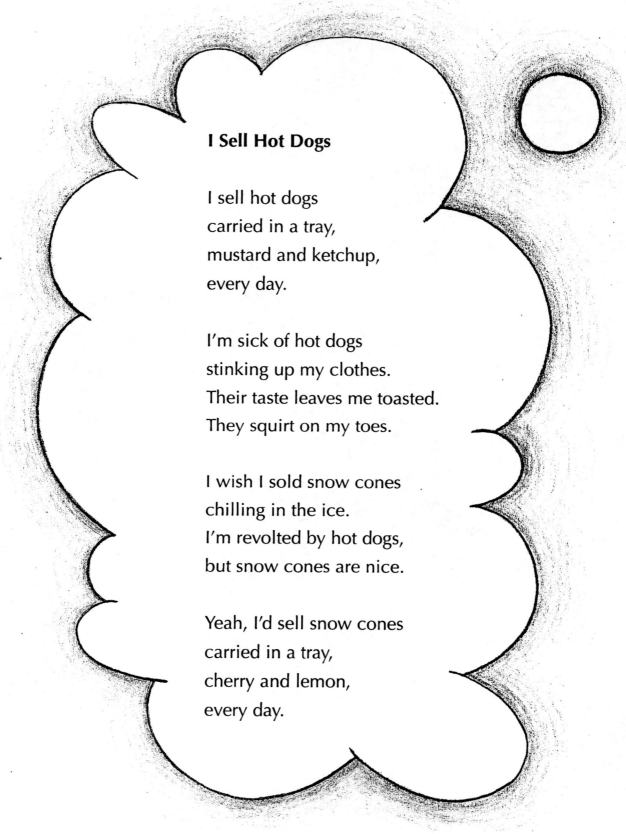

I Sell Hot Dogs

I sell hot dogs
carried in a tray,
mustard and ketchup,
every day.

I'm sick of hot dogs
stinking up my clothes.
Their taste leaves me toasted.
They squirt on my toes.

I wish I sold snow cones
chilling in the ice.
I'm revolted by hot dogs,
but snow cones are nice.

Yeah, I'd sell snow cones
carried in a tray,
cherry and lemon,
every day.

I Sell Snow Cones

I sell snow cones
carried in a tray,
cherry and lemon,
every day.

I'm sick of snow cones
staining all my clothes.
Their taste leaves me frigid.
They drip on my toes.

I wish I sold hot dogs
steaming in a bun.
I'm disgusted with snow cones,
but hot dogs are fun.

Yeah, I'd sell hot dogs
carried in a tray,
mustard and ketchup,
every day.

I Wish My Dad

I wish my dad was a circus star,
who would swing upon the trapeze.
He'd wear an outfit of dazzling gold,
not stay home to make me eat peas.

I wish my dad could do back flips
to astonish me and my brother.
This silly dream will not come true,
'cause he'll never be like my mother.

Inside the Lion's Jaws

My mother's in the cage.
She's trapped behind a fence
with cracking whips and metal chairs.
Oh, this makes me tense.

Audience, please stop your cheers.
I am the next of kin.
Although the mouth is open,
the head must not go in.

Imagine if she sneezes.
This fills my heart with dread.
Her mighty jaws will clamp right down,
and off will go his head.

Man-Eating Tigers

I fear man-eating tigers
might like my cool toys,
but I'm even more worried
they eat little boys.

I wish man-eating tigers
would eat pretty girls,
but I bet they're all worried
they'd gag on the curls.

The Unseen Pro

There is a circus pro,
who remains unseen,
but her talent prevents
a show that's obscene.

Without the great seamstress,
acrobats must dare
to parade and perform
in their underwear.

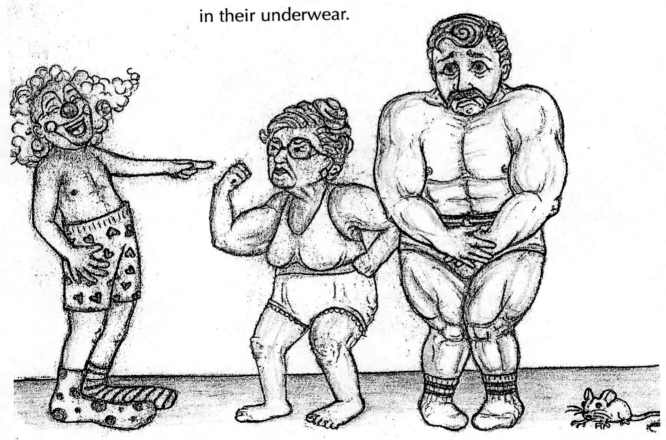

Hair Twister

The greatest star of the show
was the girl who spun by her hair.
I thought I'd give it a try,
give my friends a bit of a scare.

I tied my hair to a pole.
My best friend was really appalled.
I started spinning around,
and now I'm regrettably bald.

Dad's the Ringmaster

Lately at dinner,
he's on my nerves.
Dad tries to present
whatever Mom serves.

"Our center dish,
the baffling blend
of meats and sauces
for you, my friend.

"Plus pleasing pasta
and ice cold water,
stupendous drink
for you, my daughter.

"A final treat
will be three kisses,
a sweet reward!
Now do the dishes."

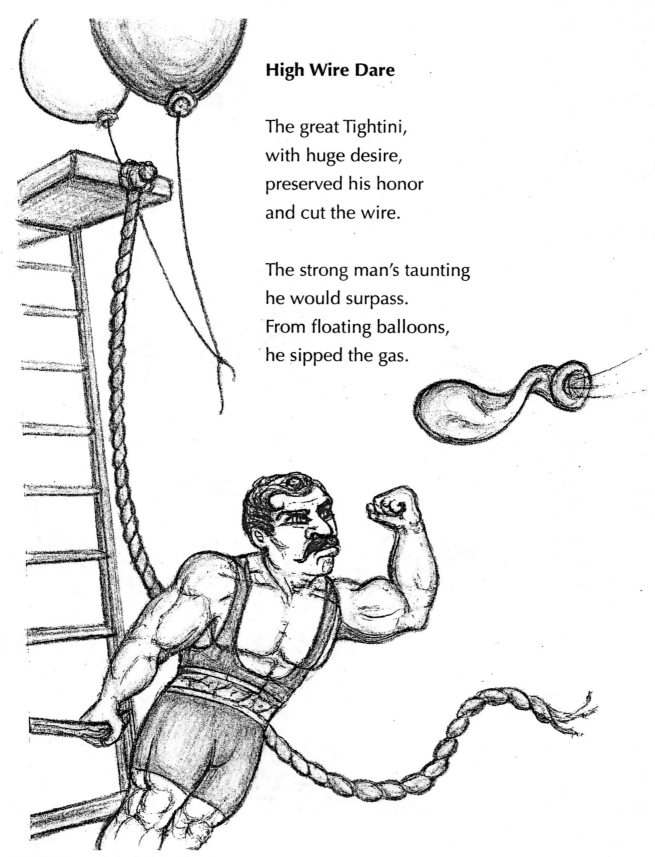

High Wire Dare

The great Tightini,
with huge desire,
preserved his honor
and cut the wire.

The strong man's taunting
he would surpass.
From floating balloons,
he sipped the gas.

His ears inflated.
His nose puffed up.
His chest expanded.
His toes swelled up.

He bowed and billowed
then took the dare
and toddled across
on just thin air.

The Human Cannonball's Last Thought   **53**

Librarian's Pet

I stood on a table.
I pinched all the girls.
I carved my initials
in fanciful swirls.

I never was quiet.
I did not read books.
I even made jokes of
librarians' looks.

When summer was over,
I won an award,
a trip to the circus.
No way I'd be bored.

Upon my arrival,
they raced to the ring
with me in a cage that
proclaimed, "WILD THING!"

The Snake Charmer

The snake charmer
with Egyptian song
woos a creature
some eight feet long.

Basket opens
without a sound;
black-eyed cobra
is soon unwound.

Slithery skin
slides like a snake,
but whiskers mean
that it's a fake.

It's not a reptile
from an ancient tomb.
It's just a mouse
in snake costume.

The Littlest Show on Earth

Posing on a pedestal,
ready, willing, and able,
skilled and daring performers
parade right on a table.

Spectators squeeze forward
to see this splendid sight,
vaulting and somersaulting,
creatures of minuscule height.

By candlelight they perform
feats of strength with ease.
Under the magnifying glass,
we see that they are fleas.

The Smallest

It's great to be small
when we climb and hop
to stack five kids high,
because I'm on top.

About the Author

J. Thomas Sparough is a professional juggler, storyteller, and facilitator. He travels the country sharing his dynamic shows for both kids and adults. He calls himself the Space Painter. He and his wife are partners in an organization called Creative Retreat LLC. Sparough is also the author of *Math Is My Bag* and *The Spiritual Exercises of the Coffee Filter*. This is his first poetry collection.

About the Illustrator

Rachael Griffin is a graduate of Ohio University, where she earned her Bachelor of Fine Arts in both printmaking and painting. Her artwork tends to use non-human imagery to provide a different perspective on specific human behaviors. This is her first book. Rachael currently resides in Hilliard, OH, with her vast pencil collection, non-stop imagination, and three hula hoops.

Space Painter Publications
4228 Delaney Street
Cincinnati, OH 45223
SpacePainter.com
(513) 542-1231

CPSIA information can be obtained at www.ICGtesting.com
Printed in the USA
LVOW09s0247150716

496402LV00008B/348/P